The
Three Little Wolves
and the
Big Bad Pig

EUGENE TRIVIZAS
ILLUSTRATED BY HELEN OXENBURY

HEINEMANN · LONDON

For Grace
E. T.

In Memory of
Stanley
H.O.

First published in Great Britain in 1993
by Heinemann Young Books
an imprint of Reed Consumer Books Limited
Michelin House, 81 Fulham Road, London SW3 6RB
and Auckland, Melbourne, Singapore and Toronto
ISBN 0 434 96050 0
A CIP catalogue record for this book is available
at the British Library
Printed in Italy
The right of Eugene Trivizas and Helen Oxenbury to
be identified as author and illustrator
of this work has been asserted by them in accordance
with the Copyright, Designs and Patents Act 1988

Once upon a time there were three cuddly little wolves with soft fur and fluffy tails who lived with their mother. The first was black, the second was grey and the third white.

One day the mother called the three little wolves round her and said, "My children, it is time for you to go out into the world. Go and build a house for yourselves. But beware of the big bad pig."

"Don't worry, Mother, we will watch out for him," said the three little wolves and they set off.

Soon they met a kangaroo who was pushing a
wheelbarrow full of red and yellow bricks.

"Please, will you give us some
of your bricks?" asked
the three little wolves.

"Certainly," said the kangaroo, and she gave them
lots of red and yellow bricks.

So the three little wolves built themselves a
house of bricks.

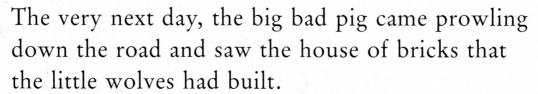

The very next day, the big bad pig came prowling
down the road and saw the house of bricks that
the little wolves had built.
The three little wolves were playing croquet
in the garden. When they saw
the big bad pig coming,
they ran inside the house
and locked the door.

The pig knocked on the door and grunted,
"Little wolves, little wolves, let me come in!"

"No, no, no," said the three little wolves. "By the hair on our chinny-chin-chins, we will not let you in, not for all the tea leaves in our china teapot!"

"Then I'll huff and I'll puff and I'll blow your house down!" said the pig.

So he huffed and he puffed and he puffed and he huffed, but the house didn't fall down.

But the pig wasn't called big and bad for nothing.
He went and fetched his sledgehammer and he
knocked the house down.

The three little wolves only
just managed to escape before the bricks
crumbled, and they were very frightened indeed.

"We shall have to build a stronger house," they said.
Just then, they saw a beaver who was mixing
concrete in a concrete mixer.

"Please, will you give us some of your concrete?"
asked the three little wolves.

"Certainly," said the beaver and he gave them buckets and buckets full of messy, slurry concrete.

So the three wolves built themselves a house of concrete.

No sooner had they finished than the big bad pig came prowling down the road and saw the house of concrete that the little wolves had built.

They were playing battledore and shuttlecock in the garden and when they saw the big bad pig coming, they ran inside their house and shut the door.

The pig rang the bell and said, "Little frightened wolves, let me come in!"

"No, no, no," said the three little wolves. "By the hair on our chinny-chin-chins, we will not let you in, not for all the tea leaves in our china teapot."

"Then I'll huff and I'll puff and I'll blow your house down!" said the pig.

So he huffed and he puffed and he puffed and he huffed, but the house didn't fall down.

But the pig wasn't called big and bad for nothing.
He went and fetched his pneumatic drill and
smashed the house down.

The three little wolves managed to escape but
their chinny-chin-chins were trembling and trembling
and trembling.

"We shall build an even stronger house," they said, because they were very determined. Just then, they saw a lorry coming along the road carrying barbed wire, iron bars, armour plates and heavy metal padlocks.

"Please, will you give us some of your barbed wire, a few iron bars and armour plates, and some heavy metal padlocks?" they said to the rhinoceros who was driving the lorry.

"Sure," said the rhinoceros and gave them plenty of barbed wire, iron bars, armour plates and heavy metal padlocks. He also gave them some plexiglass and some reinforced steel chains because he was a generous and kind-hearted rhinoceros.

So the three little wolves built themselves an extremely strong house. It was the strongest, securest house one could possibly imagine. They felt very relaxed and absolutely safe.

The next day, the big bad pig came prowling along
the road as usual. The little wolves were playing
hopscotch in the garden. When they saw the big bad
pig coming, they ran inside their house, bolted the
door and locked all the sixty-seven padlocks.

The pig pressed the video entrance phone and
said, "Frightened little wolves with the trembling
chins, let me come in!"

"No, no, no!" said the little wolves. "By the hair on our chinny-chin-chins, we will not let you in, not for all the tea leaves in our china teapot."

"Then I'll huff and I'll puff and I'll blow your house down!" said the pig.

So he huffed and he puffed and he puffed and he huffed, but the house didn't fall down.

But the pig wasn't called big and bad for nothing. He brought some dynamite, laid it against the house, lit the fuse and…

the house
blew up.

The little wolves
just managed to escape
with their fluffy tails scorched.

"Something must be wrong with our building materials," they said. "We have to try something different. But *what?*"

At that moment, they saw a flamingo bird coming along pushing a wheelbarrow full of flowers.

"Please, will you give us some flowers?" asked the little wolves.

"With pleasure," said the flamingo bird and gave them lots of flowers. So the three little wolves built themselves a house of flowers.

One wall was of marigolds, one wall of daffodils, one wall of pink roses and one wall of cherry blossom. The ceiling was made of sunflowers and the floor was a carpet of daisies. They had water lilies in their bathtub and buttercups in their fridge. It was a rather fragile house and it swayed in the wind, but it was very beautiful.

Next day, the big bad pig came prowling down the road and saw the house of flowers that the little wolves had built.

He rang the bluebell and said, "Little frightened wolves with the trembling chins and the scorched tails, let me come in!"

"No, no, no," said the three little wolves. "By the hair on our chinny-chin-chins, we will not let you in, not for all the tea leaves in our china teapot!"

"Then I'll huff and I'll puff and I'll blow your house down!" said the pig.

But as he took a deep breath, ready to huff and puff, he smelled the soft scent of the flowers. It was fantastic. And because the scent took his breath away, the pig took another breath and then another. Instead of huffing and puffing, he began to sniff.

He sniffed deeper and deeper until he was quite filled with the fragrant scent. His heart became tender and he realised how horrible he had been in the past. In other words, he became a big *good* pig. He started to sing and to dance the tarantella.

At first, the three little wolves were a bit worried, thinking that it might be a trick, but soon they realized that the pig had truly changed, so they came running out of the house. They introduced themselves and started playing games with him.

First they played pig-pog and then piggy-in-the-middle
and when they were all tired, they
invited him into the house.

They offered him china tea and strawberries
and wolfberries, and asked him to stay with
them as long as he wanted.
The pig accepted, and they all lived happily
together ever after.

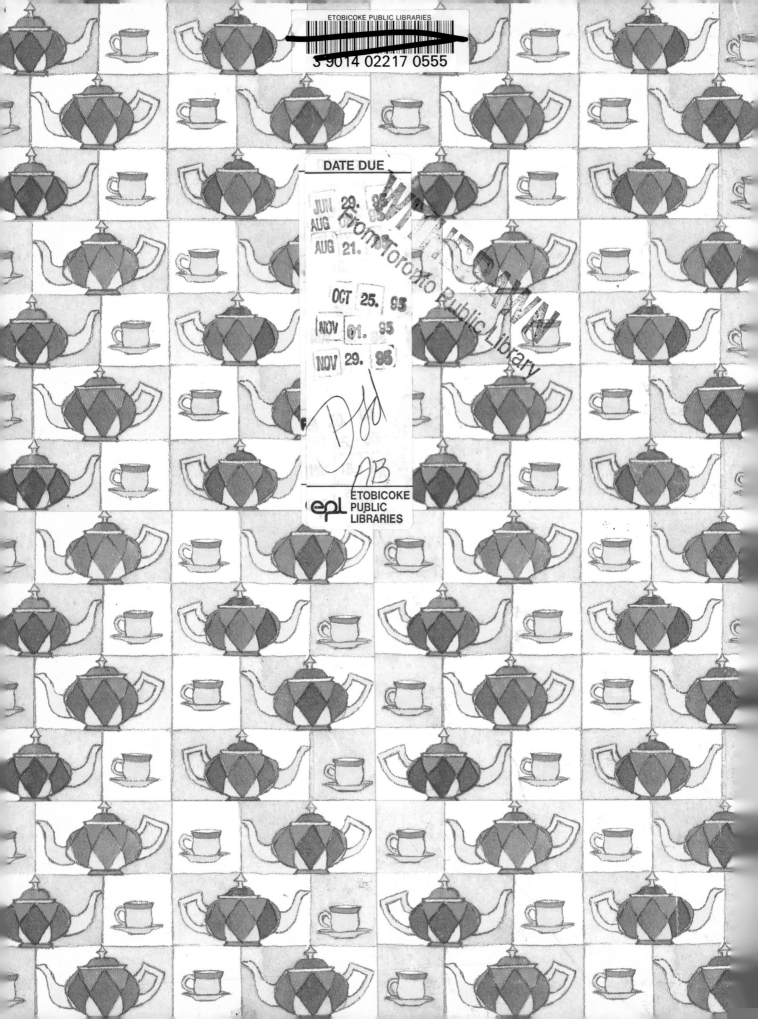

Weekly Reader Children's Book Club presents

The Book of
GIANT STORIES

by David L. Harrison

Illustrated by Philippe Fix

AMERICAN HERITAGE PRESS • NEW YORK

Text 1972 by David L. Harrison.   Pictures copyright © 1972 by Philippe Fix.
Published in 1972 by American Heritage Press, a division of McGraw-Hill Book Company.
Published in Canada by McGraw-Hill Company of Canada, Ltd.
Printed in Italy.

Library of Congress Catalog Card Number: 79-148125
(Trade) 07-026857-6   (Library) 07-026858-4

Weekly Reader Children's Book Club Edition

A careless giant once sat
On top of a very small gnat.
The gnat looked around
And said with a frown,
"That giant has ruined my hat!"

I
THE LITTLE
BOY'S SECRET

One day a little boy left school early because he had a secret to tell his mother. He was in a hurry to get home so he took a short cut through some woods where three terrible giants lived. He hadn't gone far before he met one of them standing in the path.

W hen the giant saw the little boy, he put his hands on his hips and roared, "What are you doing here, boy? Don't you know whose woods these are?"

"I'm on my way home," answered the little boy. "I have a secret to tell my mother."

That made the giant furious. "Secret?" he bellowed. "What secret?"

I can't tell you," said the little boy, "or it wouldn't be a secret anymore."

"Then I'm taking you to our castle!" said the giant. Stooping down, he picked up the little boy and plopped him into his shirt pocket.

B efore long the first giant met a second giant who was twice as big, three times as ugly, and four times as mean. "What's that in your pocket?" he asked the first giant.

"A boy," he answered. "Says he has a secret that he won't tell us."

When the second giant heard that, he laughed a wicked laugh. "Won't tell us, eh?" he chuckled. "Well, we'll just see about that! To the castle with him!"

The giants thumped on down the path. In a short time they came to a huge stone castle beside a muddy river.

At the door they met the third giant, who was five times bigger, six times uglier, and seven times meaner than the second giant.

"What's that in your pocket?" he asked the first giant.

"A boy," he answered.

"A boy!" chuckled the third giant. He brought his huge eye close to the pocket and peered in.

"Says he has a secret he won't tell us," said the first giant.

When the third giant heard that, he laughed a terrible laugh. "Won't tell us, eh?" he asked. "Well, we'll just see about that! On the table with him!"

The first giant took the little boy from his pocket and set him on the kitchen table. Then all three giants clustered around and peered down at him.

The little boy looked at the first giant. He looked at the second giant. He looked at the third giant.

They were truly enormous and quite mean-looking.

"Well?" said the first giant.

"We're waiting," said the second giant.

"I'll count to three," said the third giant. "One…two…."

The little boy sighed a big sigh.

Oh, all right," said the little boy. "I suppose I can tell you. But if I do, you must promise to let me go."

"We promise," answered the giants. But they all winked sly winks at one another and crossed their fingers behind their backs because they didn't really mean to let him go at all.

The little boy turned to the first giant. "Bend down," he said. When the giant leaned down, the little boy whispered into his ear.

When the giant heard the secret, he leaped up from the table. His knees shook. His tongue hung out. "Oh, no!" he shouted. "That's terrible!" And he dashed from the castle, ran deep into the woods, and climbed to the top of a tall tree. He didn't come down for three days.

The second giant scowled at the little boy.

"What's wrong with him?" he asked.

"Never mind," said the little boy. "Just bend down."

When that giant leaned down, the little boy stood on tiptoe and whispered into his ear.

When the giant heard the secret, he leaped up so fast that he knocked his chair over. His eyes rolled. His ears twitched. "How awful!" he roared. And he raced from the castle, ran over a hill, and crawled into the deepest, darkest cave he could find.

The third giant scowled fiercely at the little boy.

"What's wrong with them?" he asked.

"Never mind," said the little boy. "Just bend down."

When the giant leaned down, the little boy climbed onto a teacup and whispered into his ear.

When that giant heard the secret, he jumped up so fast that he ripped the seat of his trousers. His teeth chattered. His hair stood up. "Help!" he cried. "Help!" And he dashed from the castle and dived headfirst into the muddy river.

The castle door had been left open, and since the giants had promised the little boy that he could go, he walked on home.

He told his mother his secret, but she didn't yell and run away. She put him to bed and fed him some supper.

The next morning when the little boy woke up, he was covered from head to toe with bright red spots.

"Now I can tell *everybody* what my secret was," he said with a smile. "My secret was…I'M GETTING THE MEASLES!"

George the unusual giant
Never was cross or defiant,
And oddest of all,
George really was small—
He was just a peanut of a giant!

II
THE GIANT WHO WAS AFRAID OF BUTTERFLIES

There used to be a cranky witch who lived at the top of a hill in a creaky old house with eleven black cats and any number of spiders and bats.

In the valley below lived a huge giant whose thundering footsteps shook the ground when he walked around.

The witch despised the giant because every time he went walking, the ground shook so much that bats kept tumbling from her ceiling and plopping into her lap or her soup.

Sometimes the witch became so angry that she would leap onto her broom and streak down over the valley to scold the giant. But to the huge giant the witch looked no bigger than a pesky mosquito buzzing around his head. He never paid much attention to her, and that made her angrier still.

Finally the witch decided to cast an evil spell on the giant. Far into the night she stirred her bubbling pot and added witchy things like poison ivy and pigs' toes and thistles. She muttered and cackled and screeched until at last the spell was ready. Then she rolled her eyes and croaked:

Boil and bubble, witch's brew—
I'll fix that giant when I'm through.
When I've cast my evil spell,
Tomorrow he won't see so well!
My spell will play tricks on his eyes
To make things look two times his size!

The next morning the giant opened his eyes and looked to see what sort of a day it was. The first thing he saw was a squirrel scampering down a tree. Because of the witch's evil spell, the squirrel looked two times bigger than the giant.

With a frightened roar, he leaped backward and knocked down three trees.

A bird landed on the grass to hunt worms. To the bewitched giant the bird looked twice his size. This time he fell into a pond and splashed out most of the water.

Everything the poor giant saw looked bigger than he was. A butterfly scared him silly.

A dragonfly looked big enough to drag him off.

When a fuzzy caterpillar crawled toward him, the giant became so upset that he ran to the far end of the valley.

J ust then the cranky witch zoomed overhead, cackling.

"How do you like my little magic spell?" she shrieked. *"Now* perhaps you'll behave yourself and stop stomping around shaking the ground and disturbing my supper!"

To the giant the witch looked huge as she zipped around his head. Shaking with fright, he dashed out of his valley and around the far side of the hill to hide.

It happened that a small village lay on the other side of the hill. A little boy from the village was walking down the road.

When the giant saw the boy, he tripped over a farmer's barn and smashed it as flat as a dinner plate.

"Don't hurt me!" he cried. "You're bigger than I am."

"That's silly," the boy said. "I'm only a little boy. You're a great big giant."

"I know," the giant sighed. "But the witch on the hill has cast a spell on me, and now everything I see looks bigger than I am. I'm frightened by birds and worms and squirrels and butterflies and caterpillars — even little boys. I don't know what I'm going to do."

The little boy sat down beside the giant and helped him think. After a while he had an idea.

Maybe you need glasses," he told the giant. "If you wore glasses, you could see things again the way they really are. Why don't you come to the village with me and ask the eye doctor to help you?"

That idea pleased the giant very much. But as they walked along the road to town, a bee frightened him, and he accidentally kicked over a windmill.

A cow scared him so badly that he accidentally squashed a hen house.

And a puppy frightened him into knocking down several lines full of clean clothes.

"I think you'd better wait here," the boy told him. "I'll bring the glasses to you."

"All right," sighed the giant. "But do hurry." And he sat down beside the road and waited.

Soon the boy returned carrying a huge pair of glasses.
"I hope they fit," he said. "They were the biggest ones I could get."

The giant placed the glasses on his nose and squinted through them. The boy looked tiny, the way a little boy should look to a huge giant.

Birds looked no bigger than gnats.

Trees looked no bigger than grass.

The giant smiled a giant smile. "You're a good friend," he told the boy. "Now let's take a little walk up that hill!"

The giant carried the boy with him up to the witch's creaky old house.

She was not at all pleased to see them coming. "Shoo!" she shrieked. "Go away! Leave me alone!"

But the giant wasn't frightened anymore. He picked up the

witch's flying broom and snapped it between his fingers like a matchstick. With a scowl, he chased away all eleven cats. Then he let loose all the bats and spiders from the creaky old house.

Finally he snatched up the witch herself.

"Are you ready to behave yourself?" he rumbled.

"Oh, all right," she snapped. "You win. Put me down and I'll remove the spell."

And she did.

After that, the giant and the little boy often took long walks together up and down the valley. The giant's thundering footsteps still made the ground shake.

And the cranky witch still sat in her creaky old house on the hill and muttered to herself.

But when a bat plopped into her soup, she just helped it out. Never again did she try casting a spell on the little boy's giant friend.

There once was a giant named Groans,
Who lived in a castle of stones,
And often he said,
"I'd sure like some bread,
But I hate grinding up all those bones!"

III
THE GIANT
WHO THREW TANTRUMS

At the foot of Mount Thistle lay a village.

In the village lived a little boy who liked to go walking. One Saturday afternoon the little boy was walking in the woods when he was startled by a terrible noise.

He popped behind a bush.

Before long a huge giant came stamping down the path.

He looked upset.

Tanglebangled ringlepox!" the giant bellowed. He banged his head against a tree until the leaves shook off like snowflakes.

"Franglewhangled whippersnack!" the giant roared. Yanking up the tree, he whirled it around his head and knocked down twenty-seven other trees.

Muttering to himself, he stalked up the path toward the top of Mount Thistle.

The little boy hurried home.

"I just saw a giant throwing a tantrum!" he told everyone in the village.

They only smiled.

"There's no such thing as a giant," the mayor assured him.

"He knocked down twenty-seven trees," said the little boy.

"Must have been a tornado," the weatherman said with a nod. "Happens around here all the time."

The next Saturday afternoon the little boy again went walking. Before long he heard a horrible noise.

He zipped behind a tree.

Soon the same giant came storming down the path. He still looked upset.

"Pollywogging frizzlesnatch!" he hollered. Throwing himself down, he pounded the ground with both fists.

Boulders bounced like popcorn.

Scowling crossly, the giant puckered his lips into an "O."

He drew in his breath sharply. It sounded like somebody slurping soup.

"Pooh!" he cried.

Grabbing his left foot with both hands, the giant hopped on his right foot up the path toward the top of Mount Thistle.

The little boy hurried home.

That giant's at it again," he told everyone. "He threw such a tantrum that the ground trembled!"

"Must have been an earthquake," the police chief said. "Happens around here sometimes."

The next Saturday afternoon the little boy again went walking. Before long he heard a frightening noise.

He plopped behind a rock.

Soon the giant came fuming down the path. When he reached the little boy's rock, he puckered his lips into an "O." He drew in his breath sharply with a loud, soup-slurping sound. "Phooey!" he cried. "I *never* get it right!"

The giant held his breath until his face turned blue and his eyes rolled up. "Fozzlehumper backawacket!" he panted. Then he lumbered up the path toward the top of Mount Thistle.

The little boy followed him. Up and up and up he climbed to the very top of Mount Thistle.

There he discovered a huge cave. A surprising sound was coming from it. The giant was crying!

All I want is to whistle," he sighed through his tears. "But every time I try, it comes out wrong!"

The little boy had just learned to whistle. He knew how hard it could be. He stepped inside the cave.

The giant looked surprised. "How did *you* get here?"

"I know what you're doing wrong," the little boy said.

When the giant heard that, he leaned down and put his hands on his knees.

"Tell me at once!" he begged.

"You have to stop throwing tantrums," the little boy told him.

"I promise!" said the giant, who didn't want anyone thinking he had poor manners.

"Pucker your lips…" the little boy said.

"I always do!" the giant assured him.

"Then blow."
the little boy added.
"Blow?"

"Blow."

The giant looked as if he didn't believe it. He puckered his lips into an "O." He blew. Out came a long, low whistle. It sounded like a train locomotive. The giant smiled.

He shouted, "I whistled! Did you hear that? I whistled!"

Taking the little boy's hand, he danced in a circle.

"You're a good friend," the giant said.

"Thank you," said the little boy. "Sometime maybe we can whistle together. But right now I have to go. It's my suppertime."

The giant stood before his cave and waved good-by.

The little boy seldom saw the giant after that. But the giant kept his promise about not throwing tantrums.

"We never have earthquakes," the mayor liked to say.

"Haven't had a tornado in ages," the weatherman would add.

Now and then they heard a long, low whistle somewhere in the distance.

"Must be a train," the police chief would say.

But the little boy knew his friend the giant was walking up the path toward the top of Mount Thistle — whistling.

There once was a silly old witch
Who captured two frogs in a ditch.
She named one Pog,
The other one Wog,
But she never could tell which was which!